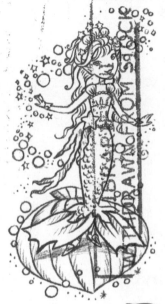

Fancy Dress Party

ROSIE BANKS

ORCHARD

This is the Secret Kingdom

Fancy Dress Party

Contents

Dance Disaster!

"You're on in a minute, Jasmine,"
Summer Hammond whispered to her
friend.

Jasmine Smith grinned. "Brilliant!" she
said. She was playing Cinderella in the
end-of-term show at school, and this
was the final dress rehearsal. The first
performance was at seven o'clock that
evening and Jasmine could hardly wait.

Their other best friend, Ellie Macdonald, was sitting with the rest of the orchestra on the other side of the stage, holding her recorder. "Good luck," she mouthed at Jasmine.

Jasmine waved, then smoothed down her costume. "Do I look okay?" she asked Summer, twirling round. She was wearing a tattered dress and a grubby white apron, and her long, dark hair was tied up under a handkerchief.

"You look perfect!" replied Summer. "Those ragged clothes are just right for Cinderella."

"Ready, everyone?" asked Mrs Benson, the girls' teacher. "Here we go." Flicking back her blonde pigtails, Summer picked up the script and opened it at the first page. She'd be prompting in case anyone forgot their lines. Summer was really happy to be behind the scenes with a book, helping her friends – she'd hate to be out on stage performing like Jasmine.

At a signal from Mrs Benson, the orchestra began to play and Jasmine ran onto the stage. Grabbing a broom, she pretended to sweep the floor. "There's so much work to do," she sighed, saying her line clearly so that even people at the back would be able to hear. Then she started her dance.

Summer watched delightedly. Jasmine had been practising the dance for weeks, and she skipped and twirled across the stage happily. Jasmine wanted to be a pop star or an actress when she grew up, and Summer knew it would be the perfect job for her.

Suddenly Jasmine caught her foot on her skirt. She stumbled, dropping the broom with a loud clatter. Then she stopped, in the middle of the stage, and stared down at the floor, breathing hard.

"Keep going," whispered Summer. The orchestra was still playing. Most of the musicians hadn't even noticed what

had happened, though Ellie had stopped
playing her recorder and was watching
Jasmine, looking worried.

Jasmine didn't move.

"Jasmine!" Summer whispered again.

Suddenly Jasmine burst into tears.
As Summer ran forward to comfort
her, Jasmine hurried off the stage. She
charged straight past the orchestra and
out of the hall. Mrs Benson waved
her baton to stop the music and Ellie
hurriedly put down her recorder and
dashed after her friend, her red curls
bouncing. Summer was close behind her.

They found Jasmine in a classroom that
had been turned into a dressing room
for the play. She was slumped in a chair
behind the costume rail, crying.

Summer and Ellie crouched down

beside her. "It's okay," said Ellie gently, putting her hand on Jasmine's arm. She hated to see her friend so upset.

"No it's not," sobbed Jasmine. "I forgot my dance."

"Only because you tripped," Summer pointed out. "You know it really."

"I'm not so sure," groaned Jasmine. She buried her face in her hands. "I'm going to tell Mrs Benson I can't do it."

Ellie and Summer exchanged anxious looks. "You can't back out now," Summer said. "The show can't happen without Cinderella!"

"It's stage fright, that's all," said Ellie. "Loads of actors feel nervous before a show, but they're fine once they get on stage."

"And think of all the things we've faced

in the Secret Kingdom," added Summer in a low voice, checking that no one was around to overhear. "Magic thunderbolts and fairytale baddies – they're much scarier than a bit of stage fright!"

Jasmine gave a weak smile as she thought about the Secret Kingdom.

It was a wonderful place full of pixies, imps, unicorns and other incredible

creatures, all ruled by kindly King Merry.
When his evil sister, Queen Malice, had
tried to take over the kingdom, he'd
made a Magic Box that had found its
way to the only people who could help
– Ellie, Summer and Jasmine. They'd
shared some amazing adventures in the
Secret Kingdom, helping to fix all the
trouble that Queen Malice had caused.

Summer took Jasmine's hands. "We
broke all of Queen Malice's horrible
thunderbolts," she reminded her. "*And*
we stopped King Merry from turning
into a stink toad. You were really brave
then, remember?"

Jasmine gave a small nod, but still
looked unsure.

"Hang on," said Ellie, jumping up. She
ran over to her school bag and pulled out

the Magic Box, which was beautifully
carved with pictures of mermaids,
unicorns and other wonderful creatures.
On the lid was a mirror surrounded
by six green gems. "Here," she said,
holding it out to Jasmine. She wished
the box would bring them a message
from Trixibelle, King Merry's pixie
assistant, but maybe just holding it would
make Jasmine feel better.
"Remember all the—" She
broke off suddenly as the mirror on the
box's lid began to glow.

   "Oh!" gasped Summer. "A message!"

   "Really?" Jasmine looked up eagerly,
quickly rubbing the tears away from her
eyes. A trip to the Secret Kingdom would
be the perfect thing to take her mind off
the show!

A Message from Trixi

Jasmine dried her eyes and sat down next to Ellie and Summer. Ellie placed the box on Jasmine's lap and the three friends stared intently at the mirror, their hearts thumping with excitement.

All of a sudden, words in beautiful curly writing appeared in the mirror:

Dear friends, please come at once, I fear
We need help with a problem here.
Please hurry to the village square
Where imps make lovely things to wear.

"One of the fairytale baddies must have turned up!" exclaimed Ellie.

Queen Malice's most recent trouble-causing plan had been to release six baddies from Summer's book of fairytales into the Secret Kingdom. The girls had already managed to capture four of them but there were still two on the loose. Ellie guessed that this message meant one of them had been spotted.

"We've got to solve the riddle quickly," said Summer. "The sooner we get to the Secret Kingdom the better!"

The Magic Box flew open to reveal six compartments, each one containing a magical treasure from the girls' adventures in the kingdom.

Summer felt a tingle of excitement run down her spine as she looked into the box. It held a glittering crystal that could control the weather, an icy hourglass that could freeze time, a tiny bag of glitter dust with enough magic left to make one wish come true, a pearl to make them invisible, and, Summer's favourite, a tiny silver unicorn horn that let them talk to animals. In the sixth compartment was a piece of folded paper – a magical map of the Secret Kingdom.

The map rose up out of the box and Ellie caught it, unfolding it carefully.

"We're looking for a village," she said, smoothing out the creases.

"Where imps live," added Summer, peering closely at the map. The map was like a window that looked down onto the Secret Kingdom, and she could see tiny figures moving about on the crescent-shaped island. "Look," she said. "There are the unicorns in their orchard."

"And there's an elf butler by King Merry's Enchanted Palace," said Ellie, watching him go in through the front door with a basket of strawberries.

"We're looking for imps who make lovely things to wear," Jasmine said, her dancing disaster forgotten. "Have we ever been to a place like that?"

"I don't think so," replied Ellie. "So we

must be going somewhere new."

They grinned excitedly. The Secret Kingdom was full of amazing places just waiting to be explored.

"I've got it!" called Jasmine, pointing to a dot on the map. "Fancy Dress Village! That must be full of lovely things to wear."

"Of course!" Ellie cried. She quickly folded the map again and put it back into its compartment. The box snapped shut, then the girls placed their hands over the green gems that surrounded the mirror. "The answer is Fancy Dress Village!" they said together.

Suddenly silvery light came streaming out of the mirror on the box's lid. It whirled around them, filling the room with sparkles, then a beautiful pixie

appeared, hovering on a
leaf. She was wearing
a dress and hat made
from yellow petals
that curled at the
edges, and shoes
made of pale
green leaves. The
tips of her pointy
ears peeked out
from her tangle

of blonde hair, and her magic pixie ring
twinkled on her finger.

"Trixi!" the girls cheered, overjoyed to
see their friend again.

"Hello, girls," Trixi said with an
unhappy sniff. The little pixie didn't look
like her usual cheerful self at all.

"What's wrong?" Summer asked

nervously. "Is there another fairytale baddie on the loose?"

"No," replied Trixi sadly. "It's something else." Her blue eyes started to fill with tears.

"What?" the girls said together, shocked to see the tiny pixie looking so unhappy.

Trixi sighed. "It's the Secret Kingdom's annual fancy dress party today. There's a prize for the best costume and I've got *nothing* to wear!" She took a little handkerchief from her pocket and dabbed her eyes. "I know it's not as important as catching fairytale baddies, but will you help me find my costume?"

"Of course we will!" Summer exclaimed, relieved that nothing terrible had happened in the Secret Kingdom.

"I really wanted to win the fancy dress crown this year," continued Trixi, blowing her nose. "Grandmother Aura, the royal costume designer, was making costumes for King Merry and me, but when I went to Fancy Dress Village this morning to collect them, she wasn't there."

"We'll find her for you, Trixi," promised Summer.

"And I bet your costume will be the best ever!" Jasmine added.

"I hope you're right," Trixi said, sounding a bit more cheerful. "The fancy dress competition is brilliant fun, I'd hate to miss it."

"Let's go, then," said Ellie. "The sooner we get there, the sooner we can find your costume."

Trixi beamed at them. "Thank you! You're such good friends, I knew I could count on you."

Ellie, Summer and Jasmine jumped up and held hands. They smiled excitedly at each other as Trixi tapped her pixie ring and chanted:

Pixie magic, don't be slow.
To Fancy Dress Village we must go!

A stream of sparkles flew out of her pixie ring and surrounded them, spinning so fast around the girls that they were lifted off their feet. They squeezed one another's hands tightly. "Wheeeee!" cried Ellie. "Secret Kingdom here we come!"

Fancy Dress Village

The girls soared high in the air, with the glittering cloud whirling around them, then felt themselves drifting slowly downwards. Landing with a gentle bump, they looked round eagerly.

They were in a cobbled square surrounded on all sides by cute thatched cottages with low doors and diamond-paned windows. "What a pretty place!" exclaimed Jasmine.

"And we're wearing our tiaras again,"
said Summer excitedly, spotting her
reflection in one of the windows. Their
beautiful jewelled tiaras that showed
they were Very Important Friends of the
Secret Kingdom always appeared the
moment they arrived.

"These houses are so sweet!" Ellie
said, running to peer inside the nearest
cottage. "Come and see," she called.

Summer and Jasmine ran after Ellie
and peeped in at the window.

A pointy-eared imp with a kind face
and sparkling green eyes was sitting at
a table inside. She was wearing a pink
dress with lacy ruffles at the neck and a
frilly hat shaped like a flower. She was
sewing the ears onto a tiger costume.

"That costume's amazing!" exclaimed

Jasmine excitedly.

"Look at the beautiful black-and-orange stripes," said Ellie.

"It looks so realistic," Summer agreed.

The imp looked up and smiled at the girls before returning to her work.

"Let's see what's happening next door," Jasmine suggested.

They ran to the next cottage where another imp was sewing a glittering horn onto a beautiful unicorn costume. His needle flashed in and out so fast that they could barely see it.

"That costume's brilliant, too," said Ellie, impressed.

"All the imps who live in Fancy Dress Village make amazing costumes," Trixi told them. "And when they're finished, they sew costume magic into them."

"*Costume* magic?" asked Summer. "What does that do?"

"Wait and see!" Trixi giggled.

Summer peeped in at another window where an imp with yellow hair was working on a fluffy pink-and-lilac striped bubblebee costume. "These costumes look amazing!" she said. "No wonder you were so upset when you couldn't find yours, Trixi."

"Grandmother Aura makes the best costumes of all," Trixi said with a smile. "Come on, she lives over here. Perhaps she's there now."

Trixi sped across the square on her leaf, her blonde hair streaming out behind her, followed by the girls. Ellie looked longingly at the little thatched cottages surrounding the square. "I wish we had time to look in at all the windows," she said. "I love seeing what the imps are making."

Grandmother Aura's cottage stood on one corner of the square. It had bright blue shutters and a matching front door,

with a brass knocker shaped like a bird. Jasmine knocked on the door. No one answered, but the door swung open.

"Do you think Grandmother Aura would mind if we went in?" Summer asked.

Trixi shook her head. "I'm sure she wouldn't."

"Maybe we'll find a clue about where she is," Jasmine added.

"Look at all this!" exclaimed Ellie as they went inside. The front room of the cosy cottage had been turned into a bright workshop. One wall was lined with shelves holding jars of glittering sequins, bright beads and buttons, and reels of silky ribbon and colourful thread. Another wall was covered in animal masks, and hats decorated with

enormous curly feathers. There were rails
bursting with beautiful costumes against
all the other walls. "Wow!" Ellie gasped.

"She must have left in a hurry – this costume's half-finished," said Jasmine, noticing a gorgeous peacock costume on a table near the window that had half its feathers missing. "I wonder where she's gone?"

Just then there was a weak cough from the next room. Trixi quickly flew her leaf over to a door at the back of the workshop and opened it a crack. "Grandmother Aura!" she called in surprise. "Are you here?"

"I'm in bed," a quavery, high-pitched voice called back. "Don't come in."

The girls rushed over and peered inside. The curtains were closed, making the room dark and dingy, but the girls could make out a bed with posts carved in the shape of tall flowers.

Grandmother Aura lay under the blankets, completely hidden from sight. "I'm afraid I've got a bad case of imp-itis," she sighed. "But the costumes you wanted are in my workshop, Trixi, on the shelf beside the door."

"Oh, thank you!" Trixi cried excitedly. "I hope you feel better soon!" She beamed at the girls, then steered her leaf over to some tall shelves at one side of the workshop. The shelves were piled high with beautifully-wrapped presents, and each one had a label tied with a colourful ribbon.

"Here's yours, Trixi!" said Ellie. The tiny parcel with Trixi's name on it was wrapped with shiny gold paper and crimson ribbon.

Eagerly, Trixi carried it over to the table beside the window. The girls gathered round to watch as she slipped off the ribbon and tore open the paper. "Wow!" she gasped. There was a tiny mermaid costume inside.

"It's gorgeous, Trixi!" exclaimed Summer. She carefully picked up the little tail, which was covered in glittering green-and-blue scales.

"And there's even a shell costume to

cover your leaf," added Jasmine.

"It's perfect," Trixi said, turning
a somersault on her leaf in delight.
She tapped her glittery pixie ring and
surrounded herself with turquoise
sparkles. As they cleared, she was
wearing the mermaid outfit.
Her blonde hair was
tucked under a hat
made of bubbles, but
when she took it
off the girls gasped.
Trixi's usually
short hair hung in
beautiful long curls
to her waist, and
a gorgeous shell
headband held it back
from her face.

"You look lovely, Trixi!" cried Ellie. "And your hair's so long!"

"Thanks!" Trixi flicked her curls delightedly, and wriggled her shimmering tail. "That must be the costume magic Grandmother Aura sewed into my costume – it's made my hair long, just like a mermaids'! If I was in water now, I'd be able to swim like a mermaid, too." She flew across the room on her shell-leaf and a trail of silver bubbles streamed out behind her.

The girls laughed and reached out to catch the bubbles, but they popped the moment they touched them.

"I wish we had costumes, too," said Summer wistfully. "I love dressing up."

Trixi grinned round. "Well, I've got a surprise for you all," she said, her eyes twinkling. "I didn't want to tell you in case we couldn't find them – but I asked Grandmother Aura to make costumes for you as well!"

"For us?" gasped Ellie. "Wow!"

"You can be in the fancy dress competition too, if you like," Trixi added.

The girls exchanged excited looks. "That would be brilliant," said Summer. She couldn't wait to see what her costume was – whatever it was, it was sure to be something magical!

Costume
Magic

"That one's your costume, Summer," said Trixi, pointing at a yellow parcel tied with a turquoise ribbon.

"Thank you so much, Trixi!" Summer quickly tore away the wrapping and found a white leotard with fluffy white ears, black whiskers and a long white tail. "A cat costume!" she cried delightedly.

"That's perfect for someone who loves animals as much as you, Summer!" Jasmine smiled.

Ellie's name was on the next parcel. It was wrapped in green paper and tied with a purple ribbon. "It feels lumpy," she said curiously. "I wonder what's inside."

She ripped open the paper, then burst out laughing. "I'm going to be a clown!" She held up the red-and-yellow costume, which was covered in brightly-coloured spots.

There was a pointy purple hat with a flower coming out of the top, huge pink shoes, a red-and-white striped ruff to go round her neck and six juggling balls. "This is great!" she giggled. "Thank you, Trixi."

The third parcel looked very untidy. Its pink wrapping paper was torn and the red ribbon was loose. Jasmine's name was written on it in scruffy, uneven letters.

"Whatever's happened to it?" asked Trixi in astonishment. "Grandmother Aura is usually very careful."

"Perhaps she was trying to finish it in a
hurry," suggested Ellie.

"And she's not feeling very well, don't
forget," added Summer.

Jasmine picked up the parcel hesitantly.

"It's only the wrapping paper that's
spoiled," Ellie said. "I'm sure your
costume will be okay."

"It's not that," Jasmine replied with
a sigh. "Looking at these costumes has
made me remember the school play —
and messing up my dance."

"Try not to think about it," Summer
said, giving her a hug. "Just enjoy being
here in the Secret Kingdom."

Jasmine smiled weakly. "I'm trying.
But I can't help worrying about tonight's
performance."

"You'll be fine," Ellie reassured her.

"Now, let's unwrap your costume."

Jasmine nodded and squared her shoulders. "You're right," she said. "I don't want to spoil our time here by worrying about something back home." Laying the parcel on the bench, she tore the paper open and pulled out a ballerina's sparkly pink tutu. Her tummy flipped over. A dancer was the very last thing she wanted to be right now!

Summer and Ellie could see her disappointment. "It's very pretty," Summer said, trying to cheer her up. She hugged Jasmine again. "You'll look lovely in it."

Jasmine noticed that Trixi was watching her with a puzzled expression on her face. She forced a smile. "Thanks, Trixi. It's gorgeous," she said.

Trixi's face lit up. "Oh, good! I'm so glad you all like your costumes."

"What sort of magic's in them, Trixi?" asked Ellie, but before Trixi could reply there was a loud crash from outside.

"Help! Stop!" a voice yelled.

"What was that?" gasped Summer.

Trixi turned pale. "I think it was King Merry," she said anxiously.

"Come on!" cried Ellie. "It sounds like he needs our help!"

Something Extra Special

The girls and Trixi raced outside. In the middle of the village square, two imps were looking at a pile of costumes in amazement.

"What happened?" Jasmine asked breathlessly as she ran up to them.

"I don't know," one of the imps replied. "We were just taking these costumes to my workshop so I could finish them before the contest, when something dropped out of the sky!"

"Oh dearie, dearie me," came a voice from under the pile.

"King Merry!" Summer cried. She, Jasmine and Ellie rushed forward and started moving the clothes.

"Are you all right, Your Majesty?" gasped Summer as she picked up a feather headdress and found the little king lying in a heap.

"I don't know," came the muffled reply.

"I took my rainbow slide to get to Fancy
Dress Village, but now I don't know
where I've ended up."

"You're in Fancy Dress Village," Ellie
giggled, "but you fell on top of some
costumes!"

"Can you help?" asked King Merry.
"I'm all in a tangle."

"Of course, Your Majesty," Jasmine
said. She was glad to have something to
take her mind off the ballerina costume.

The girls pulled the clothes aside, but
when King Merry stood up, it was all
they could do not to laugh! Somehow
he'd managed to get his arms through
the straps of a pair of glittery fairy wings.
They were fluttering prettily on his back,
as though they were about to lift him
into the air. As he turned round they saw

that a large Viking helmet was jammed
on his bottom!

"Something's got me!" he
cried, straining his
neck to look over
his shoulder. "And
I can't see what it
is because I've lost
my glasses."

"It's a helmet,
Your Majesty," said
Summer with a giggle.

"And some fairy wings," Jasmine
added, struggling to keep a straight
face. She and Summer took hold of the
helmet's horns and yanked it off. Then
they helped him slide his arms out of the
wings' straps, while Ellie searched for the
missing glasses under the costumes.

"Thank you," said King Merry smoothing his ruffled hair and readjusting his crown, which had slipped over one ear.

"Here are your glasses, Your Majesty," Ellie said, pulling out a pair of half-moon spectacles from under a sailor's hat. She handed them to him.

"Excellent!" King Merry put them on. He looked closely at the girls. "Oh, hello girls! Have you come for the fancy dress party?"

"Yes," Summer said. "And Trixi's got us some great costumes to wear."

"Marvellous," said King Merry, beaming at them. "Your costume looks lovely, Trixi. If I didn't know it was you, I'd have thought you were a real mermaid. A very small one, of course."

He looked over at Grandmother Aura's cottage. "I wonder what costume Grandmother Aura has made for me this year?"

As they headed back over to Grandmother Aura's cottage, the girls explained about the poorly imp. They raced through the workshop and knocked on the bedroom door.

"Grandmother Aura, King Merry's here," Jasmine called.

King Merry peered through the doorway. "How are you, dear lady?" he asked kindly. "You mustn't overdo it. Although it would be terrible if I didn't have a costume," he added to Jasmine, Ellie and Summer in a whisper.

"I've got your costume right here, Your Majesty," called Grandmother Aura from her bed. "It's my best one yet – a wolf costume."

"A wolf costume! Excellent!" said King Merry. "I'll have to start practicing my growl."

"I'll help you get ready," Trixi told the king.

"No!" Grandmother Aura called out. "I'll help the king. There may be a few last minute adjustments."

"See you at the contest," King Merry said happily.

As the kindly king went into Grandmother Aura's room, Ellie beckoned urgently to Summer, Jasmine and Trixi.

"What's up?" asked Jasmine.

"Isn't a wolf one of the fairytale baddies that we haven't captured yet?"

Ellie whispered anxiously.

"Yes, the Big Bad Wolf." Summer shuddered, remembering the story in her fairy tale book.

"So?" asked Jasmine, puzzled.

"Did you ask Grandmother Aura to make King Merry a wolf costume, Trixi?" Ellie continued.

"No, it was a surprise. He judges the contest every year, and he likes to dress up as a different animal each time." Trixi giggled. "Last year he dressed as a rabbit, but he kept forgetting what he was and roaring like a tiger."

Summer laughed, but Jasmine looked serious. "I see what Ellie means. It seems a bit funny that King Merry's going to dress up as a wolf while there's a *real* one on the loose."

"Has anyone spotted the Big Bad Wolf, Trixi?" asked Jasmine.

"No," Trixi said, smiling. "But you don't need to worry. I'm sure someone would have noticed if he was up to something."

"I suppose you're right," said Ellie.

"And a wolf *costume* can't hurt anyone," Summer added. "So it won't matter if King Merry dresses up as one."

The girls smiled, relieved.

"Shall we change into our costumes now?" Ellie asked, picking up her clown's hat eagerly.

"Oh, yes! Let's get ready," said Summer. She looked out of the window at the village square. "And quickly! People are already starting to arrive!"

Beautiful
Costumes!

"Are you happy about wearing your costume now, Jasmine?" Summer asked as she changed into her cat outfit.

Jasmine smiled. "Yes. I don't want to be the only one not dressing up!" She pulled on her tutu, then sat down to tie the ribbons of her ballet shoes.

"Look!" cried Summer delightedly. As she put on her costume her cat tail began to swish magically and her ears and whiskers waggled happily. "There must be loads of magic in my costume."

"And mine," Ellie said, juggling six balls at once without dropping any of them. She walked up and down, her enormous pink shoes flapping. "These shoes are the funniest things ever!" She fell over, did a neat forward roll and leaped up again. "I love being a clown!"

Jasmine looked at Ellie and gave a snort of laughter. "That's not the only thing your costume magic has done," she giggled.

"What? Why?" asked Ellie.

Summer turned Ellie round so she could see her reflection in Grandmother Aura's window.

Ellie burst out laughing as she saw herself. Her nose had turned round and red, just like a clown's! She pulled off her hat and the red nose disappeared, then reappeared again when she put the hat back on.

Jasmine finished fastening her ballet shoes and stood up. She began to spin on one foot, holding her other leg out behind her and arching her arms above her head. "My costume's full of magic, too!" she exclaimed. "Look how well I can dance!"

"Beautiful!" Trixi grinned, spinning on her shell–leaf and surrounding Jasmine with bubbles.

"Look, there's Aunt Maybelle," cried Ellie, pointing outside as a group of pixies in fancy dress came flying into the square, chattering happily. Trixi and the girls rushed outside to join them. Aunt Maybelle was dressed as a cloud imp, and her leaf had transformed to look like a fluffy white cloud.

"And there's my friend, Willow," said Trixi excitedly, spotting a fairy dressed as a laughing bird.

More and more magical creatures crowded into the village. A stage had been set up in the middle of the square, and the girls grinned as they saw a golden throne in the centre of it.

"That's where the Fancy Dress King or Queen sits," Trixi explained as a group of elves hoisted up a red velvet curtain at the back of the stage, behind the throne. "Once King Merry picks the winner, they get to wear the winner's crown for the rest of the party!"

"I don't know how King Merry's ever going to choose, the costumes are all so beautiful," Summer said, pointing to a group of elves dressed as sequinned butterflies. They fluttered up into the air, making their sequins flash in the sunshine.

"I'd better go and check on King Merry," Trixi said. "He's probably got his paws on the wrong feet and his wolfy whiskers in a muddle!"

Trixi flew her leaf off towards Grandmother Aura's cottage, leaving a trail of bubbles behind her. The girls gazed around excitedly. There were amazing costumes everywhere!

"Look at that gnome!" giggled Jasmine. He was dressed as a chocolate birthday cake and wore a hat covered in candles.

"Mmm, his costume even *smells* of chocolate," Ellie said, sniffing deeply as he walked past.

A group of imps came skipping into the square. They were dressed in red and yellow jester costumes, with jingling bells on their hats and shoes.

A tiny elf ran up to her, dressed as a strawberry, and behind her came more elf children dressed as pieces of fruit. "An apple," giggled Summer. "And an orange."

"A raspberry and a banana," Jasmine said.

"And some grapes," added Ellie.

The elves raced round them in a circle. "We're a joint entry," one of them said, grinning cheekily. He signalled to his friends and they ran into a huddle, linking arms. "Can you guess what we're called?" they asked.

The girls shook their heads.

"Fruit salad!" whooped the excited children. They dashed off through the square, chuckling.

"I'm really glad Trixi brought us here,"

said Jasmine. "It's so colourful and busy."

"And everyone's cheerful," added
Ellie, waving at a brownie dressed as a
shooting star.

Willow, Trixi's fairy friend, flew over.
"Hello," she said, smiling. "Do you like
my laughing bird costume?" She flew
round in a circle so they could see the
deep blue feathery wings that completely
covered her own fairy wings, and the
feathery cap that hid her blonde hair.
"And listen to this," she said. Opening
the yellow paper beak that she wore over
her nose, she gave a cute giggling call
just like a laughing bird.

"That's great!" cried Jasmine. She
was about to ask Willow to do it again,
when something caught her eye. "Look!"
she cried, pointing at Grandmother

Aura's cottage.

A shaggy grey wolf was walking out
into the square. He had rough-
looking fur and long
claws, and he was
wearing a purple
cloak trimmed
with white
feathers.

"There's King
Merry," said
Summer. "But he's
still wearing his cloak! You look
great, Your Majesty," she called.

"Thank you, my dear," growled King
Merry, showing sharp white teeth.

The girls looked at each other in
surprise as he passed them. "I suppose
that's the magic in his costume working,"

Ellie said, "but he sounds really gruff and growly."

"I'd be afraid of him if I didn't know it was King Merry!" Summer said.

They watched him stalk away. When he reached the crowd, he barged through, knocking over an elf dressed like a cupcake. "What's he doing?" Jasmine cried furiously. "He didn't even stop to help that poor elf up!"

"He doesn't seem like himself at all," said Summer, shocked. "I don't think even one of Grandmother Aura's brilliant costumes could change him *that* much."

Ellie frowned. "Either he's a really good actor or..." She stared at Summer and Jasmine, her eyes wide with horror.

"Or it's not King Merry!" gasped Summer. "It's a real wolf!"

The Real King Merry

"It must be the Big Bad Wolf out of the fairytale book, pretending to be King Merry!" Jasmine cried.

The wolf climbed up onto the stage and gave a loud growl. "The competition is about to start," he announced. "Line up so I can judge your costumes."

Chattering excitedly, all the magical creatures skipped into line in front of the stage.

"But *why* is he pretending to be King Merry?" Summer asked.

"I don't know," said Ellie, "but I bet he's up to no good!"

"We have to put him back in the book." Jasmine said. "Where's Trixi?"

The girls looked round in dismay. Trixi had shrunk the fairytale book and put it in her pocket to keep it safe – but the little pixie was nowhere to be seen!

"I haven't seen her since she went to check on King Merry," Summer said. "The real one, I mean!"

"They must be together," said Ellie. "Quick, let's go to Grandmother Aura's."

The girls raced back to the cottage and threw open the door.

"King Merry, are you here?" called Jasmine.

"Trixi!" Summer yelled.

They all held their breath, listening for a response. "There!" cried Ellie. "What was that?"

"I didn't hear anything," Summer said.

"Trixi!" Jasmine called again.

This time they all heard it – a muffled cry coming from the back room. "In here!" Jasmine cried, throwing open the door to Grandmother Aura's bedroom.

They dashed inside and looked around. "Try the wardrobe," Ellie suggested.

There was a key in the lock. Jasmine turned it hurriedly and jumped back as the door burst open – and King Merry, Trixi and an elderly imp fell out in a heap.

The girls helped them up. "Are you okay?" Summer asked anxiously.

"Thank you, yes," said King Merry.

"Thanks to you!" Trixi added.

"And you, Grandmother Aura?" King Merry asked, turning to the imp.

She smoothed down her wispy grey hair. "I am now," she said, her kind face wrinkling as she smiled at the girls.

"Let me introduce Ellie, Jasmine and Summer," said King Merry. "They're Very Special Friends to the Secret Kingdom and they've helped us out lots of times when we've been in trouble. Girls, this is the *real* Grandmother Aura."

"Oh, thank goodness you're here, girls," Grandmother Aura said. "I've had such a terrible day. I was sewing up the hem of a ballerina costume this morning

– your costume, Jasmine – when a wolf marched in! He made me find paper and ribbon to wrap the costume in. But my hands were shaking so badly, I could hardly manage it."

"That explains why your parcel looked so untidy, Jasmine," Ellie gasped.

"Then the wolf bundled me into the wardrobe," continued Grandmother Aura. "Later, I heard you all arrive. I tried to call out, but you couldn't hear me."

The girls looked at each other in horror. "So it was the wolf who was talking to us from the bedroom!" they cried.

"Now the wolf's pretending to be King Merry," Ellie said. "Trixi, we need the book."

Suddenly, Jasmine noticed that King Merry's crown looked different from normal. He usually had a golden crown with little points on it, each topped with a precious jewel. But this one looked funny somehow. "What's happened to your crown, Your Majesty?" she asked.

King Merry took it off and looked at it in astonishment.

Summer reached out to touch it. "It's made of cardboard!" she gasped. "And the jewels aren't nearly as sparkly as the ones in your real crown."

"That's because they're costume jewels," Grandmother Aura said gravely. "That crown is the prize for the winner of the fancy dress contest."

"What...why...But where's my proper crown?" asked King Merry in a shaky voice. "I can't rule the Secret Kingdom without it."

The girls exchanged anxious looks. "The wolf must have it," said Jasmine. "We've got to get it back!"

They sprinted back across the village square, Trixi zooming alongside them, with King Merry and Grandmother Aura following behind.

The wolf was sitting on the throne in the middle of the stage. He was staring at the fancy dress contestants, his gaze moving slowly along the line.

The girls overheard an elf, standing nearby, talking to his friend. "King Merry doesn't seem like his normal self," he commented. "He's been sitting like that for ages, not talking to everyone like he usually does. It's like he's looking for someone."

"I bet I know who it is," whispered Jasmine. "There's only one person who would want to steal King Merry's crown. Queen Malice!"

The Wolf's Winner

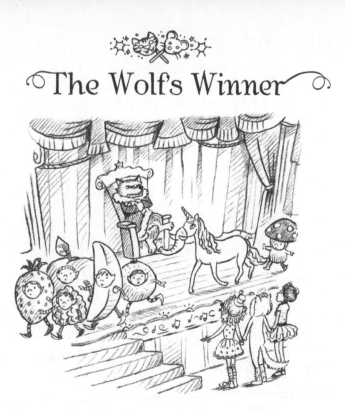

"What will happen if the wolf gives Queen Malice the crown, Trixi?" asked Summer.

"She'll rule the Secret Kingdom," Trixi replied in a shocked voice. "And then no one, not even King Merry, will be able to stop her from doing whatever she likes."

"Let's put the wolf back in the book," Jasmine suggested.

Trixi shook her head. "We can't until we find out what he's done with King Merry's crown."

"So we'll just have to stop Queen Malice from getting it first," Ellie said determinedly.

"If Queen Malice is here, we've got to find her before the wolf does," agreed Summer.

The girls and Trixi hurried past the line of contestants, trying to spot the evil queen. "What would she dress up as?" asked Ellie.

"I don't know," Summer said. "But we know she's tall so we don't need to look at the tiniest people here."

"But she might have used magic to

shrink herself," Jasmine reasoned.

"I hadn't thought of that!" groaned Summer.

"We should split up," Jasmine suggested.

"Good idea," agreed Ellie. "I'll start at the other end of the line." She dashed off, hoping desperately that they'd find Queen Malice before it was too late!

"I'll start searching in the middle," said Jasmine. "Summer, can you and Trixi check out this end of the line?"

"Okay," Summer said. "I'll wave if I spot her."

Jasmine sped away and Summer began to work her way along the line of fancy dress competitors. She passed an imp dressed as a red-and-white spotty toadstool, a fairy in a cute ladybird

costume and a brownie wearing a blue
wizard's robe decorated with silver
moons and stars.

She walked slowly along the line,
staring at every face and hoping she'd
recognise Queen Malice if she saw her.

Jasmine was rushing down the line,
too. She passed the elephant-unicorn
they'd seen earlier, and the fruit salad elf

children. Next to them were six brownies wearing colourful gnome outfits, with pointed hats and curly white beards. *I wonder if Queen Malice has disguised herself as one of them*, Jasmine thought. With their hats pulled down low over their eyebrows and their bushy beards hiding the lower parts of their faces, it wasn't easy to see who they were. She moved a little closer and the brownies beamed at her. "Do you like our

costumes?" one of them asked.

"They're great," said Jasmine. Then she smiled and moved on. Queen Malice might be able to change the way she looked, but she'd never manage to be as cheerful as the brownies!

Ellie walked slowly along the line, too, peering closely at everyone. She spotted the cupcake elf who'd been knocked over by the wolf and was glad to see him giggling with a friend dressed as a unicorn with a bright blue horn. *He wasn't badly hurt then,* she said to herself. *That's good.*

Suddenly, she noticed a beautiful dream dragon costume. The dragon's huge head had a short mane and bushy eyebrows, and its body was a length of shimmering purply-blue cloth that

hung almost to the ground. She stopped
and stared, fascinated by the way the
costume gleamed in the sunshine.

"Stop
nudging me!"
hissed a cross voice.

"You started it!" replied another.

The voices were coming from inside the
dream dragon! Ellie crouched down to
see if she could see under the costume. As
she looked, she noticed three small pairs
of legs poking out. And under the head
was someone else – somebody wearing
a black dress that swept the ground.

The dragon costume was hiding Queen
Malice and her Storm Sprites!

"Summer! Jasmine! Trixi! Over here!"
Ellie hissed, waving furiously at her
friends. "I've found her!"

But it looked as though someone
else had spotted the dream dragon,
too. Up on the stage, the wolf sprung
off the throne, his eyes gleaming with
excitement.

"Whoops!" Ellie gasped as the wolf

looked at the dream dragon and gave a
cruel grin.

Jasmine and Summer came charging
over to Ellie, with Trixi zooming along
behind them. "Queen Malice and her
Storm Sprites are inside the dream
dragon costume," Ellie whispered.

But before they could do anything
the wolf strode to the front of the stage.
"The winner is the dream dragon," he
announced in a loud, growly voice.

The dream dragon's head barged past
the girls, the Storm Sprites in the body
running to keep up.

"Stop them!" cried Jasmine, hoping
that the crowd would keep the wicked
queen away from the stage. "The wolf is
a fairytale baddie and the dream dragon
is Queen Malice and her Storm Sprites!"

The crowd burst into noisy shrieks and cries of fear. A few people bravely stood in the dream dragon's way, but they were pushed aside as the dream dragon climbed up the steps onto the stage, heading for the throne.

Suddenly Queen Malice threw off the
costume, revealing her long black dress
and her dark frizzy hair. The Storm
Sprites flew up into the air, crowing with
excitement.

"Too late, I win!"
the wicked queen
shrieked. She
sat down on
the throne,
her face
triumphant.
Then her dark
eyes glittered
with excitement

as the wolf brought out King Merry's
crown from underneath the throne. The
wolf held up the crown to show the
crowd. "Soon this will belong to the

rightful ruler of the Secret Kingdom," he
growled. "Queen Malice!"

There was a horrified gasp from the
crowd. "We've got to get the wolf back
into the fairytale book!" cried Ellie.

"Crown me!" shrieked Queen Malice.

Trixi pulled the tiny book out of her
pocket and placed it on Summer's hand.
It was no bigger than a postage stamp.
The book immediately started to grow
back to its normal size.

"Quick!" cried Jasmine. "We've got to
get closer to the wolf."

As the wolf marched towards Queen
Malice, holding the crown high, the girls
raced round to the back of the stage,
behind the velvet curtain.

Ellie pulled back the heavy fabric and
they looked out onto the stage. From

there, all they could see was Queen Malice's frizzy black hair sticking up over the back of the throne.

Summer flicked through the book, desperately searching for the right page.

"Crown me, you fool!" screeched Queen Malice.

"Yes, Your Majesty," the wolf growled. He stood behind the throne and raised King Merry's crown high above the queen's head.

"It's too late!" Ellie groaned. "We're not going to capture him in time!"

Crown or Clown?

"Got it!" cried Summer as she found the page that showed a blank, wolf-shaped space. But the wolf was already lowering King Merry's crown towards Queen Malice's head.

"Quick!" cried Jasmine.

Bravely, Summer stepped forward with the book. Ropes of light came streaking out and the girls watched anxiously as they circled the wolf. Would the magic work in time?

The wolf froze with the crown poised just above Queen Malice's frizzy hair. He looked at the light in surprise, then growled as it closed in tight around him. As he was drawn back into the book, Jasmine grabbed the crown out of his paws. The wolf struggled, but the pull of the book was too strong. With a howl of despair, the wolf was sucked back into the book, and Summer closed it with a snap.

Jasmine ducked back behind the
curtain. "That was close," she gasped,
hugging the crown tight.

Queen Malice hadn't noticed the
fuss behind her. "Crown meeee!" she
bellowed.

One of her Storm Sprites flew down,
his black wings flapping. Your Majesty,"
he warned. "The wolf's—"

"Not now!" raged the queen. She
pushed the Storm Sprite away and he
flew up into the air again.

"Hang on, I've got an idea," Ellie said.
Grinning at her friends, she wriggled
under the curtain and jumped up onto
the stage behind Queen Malice. The
others peered under the material to see
what she was up to. Taking off her
clown's hat, Ellie tiptoed up behind

the throne and held the hat above the queen's head.

Putting on a gruff, growly voice like the wolf's, she said, "I pronounce you... *Clown* Malice!" She placed her clown hat on Queen Malice's head, then, giggling, she ducked behind the curtain again.

"Look at me!" the queen cackled, leaping to her feet with her arms outstretched. "I am your queen and you will all bow to me!"

The crowd began to laugh.

"What are you all laughing at?" she shrieked. "Stop it!"

But the crowd laughed louder than ever. "Lovely nose!" called a young elf.

The girls peered round the curtain and quickly saw what everyone was finding

so funny. Queen Malice's nose was big
and red, just like a clown's!

Ellie, Summer and Jasmine started to giggle.

Queen Malice whipped her head round to look behind her. "You!" she spat as she saw the girls. She raised a hand to her head and grabbed the clown's hat. "What?" she yelled. "This isn't my crown!" Throwing it down, she stamped on it in disgust.

"This isn't yours either," Jasmine shouted, holding up the crown. "It's King Merry's."

"You're wrong!" the queen screeched. "Very soon that crown will be mine!" She thumped her thunderbolt staff down hard on the stage and a black thundercloud began to grow overhead, swelling quickly until it blotted out the sunshine.

The queen stepped onto it. "You may have captured my wolf," she hissed, "but my last fairytale baddie is the worst one of all. You'll never defeat it! Never!"

Then the storm cloud shot away, taking Queen Malice and her Storm Sprites with it.

The Fancy Dress Party

Jasmine spotted King Merry in the crowd and waved the crown in the air. "Your Majesty," she called. "We've got your crown."

The crowd parted and he came towards her, beaming. "Thank you, girls." He smiled. "You've saved the Secret Kingdom from my wicked sister again. What would we do without you?"

The crowd cheered and a group
of brownies began to dance with
excitement, swinging each other round
and skipping from foot to foot.

"Thank goodness Queen Malice's plan
didn't work," said Trixi.

The king climbed the steps to the stage.
"Friends," he said, putting on his crown.
"We're here for the fancy dress party and
we won't let my sister's bad behaviour
stop us from enjoying ourselves."

"You should enjoy yourself too, King
Merry," said Grandmother Aura. "Your
real costume is in my workroom."

"I can help with that," said Trixi. She
tapped her pixie ring and chanted:

Bring King Merry's costume here
So he can join the fun this year!

Purple sparkles shot out of the ring
and spun around King Merry. The
next moment, he was dressed in a cute
costume with a pink nose, round ears
and a long pink tail. "Eek!" he squeaked.
"I'm a mouse!"
He scurried
round the stage
happily, his
nose twitching
and his long
tail swishing
from side to side
so much that he
tripped over it, and
fell on the floor with a bump!

The girls helped him up. "Thank you,"
he said, smiling. "Tails can be tricky
things if you're not used to them. Now,

thanks to Summer, Jasmine and Ellie, the competition can begin!"

Everyone raced back to their places in front of the stage. The girls squeezed into the line of contestants between Aunt Maybelle and Willow. King Merry walked slowly across the stage with his mouse tail looped over his arm. He peered through his half-moon glasses at the costumes. "You all look wonderful," he said, beaming. "But the winner is… Trixi!"

"Me?" Trixi gasped, turning pink with excitement. "Yippee!" she whooped flying her leaf in a happy loop-the-loop.

"Well done, Trixi!" the girls said.

The tiny pixie flew over to King Merry, then looked out at the crowd. "Grandmother Aura made my costume," she said, "so I'd like her to have the crown. Besides," she added with a giggle, "it's a bit too big for me!"

"Thank you, Trixi," said Grandmother Aura, climbing up beside her. She sat on the throne and King Merry placed the cardboard crown on her head. "Two worthy winners!" he announced.

Everyone clapped and cheered.

"That was fun," said Summer as Trixi flew over to them. "Well done for winning, Trixi."

"Thanks," Trixi said. "And thanks for catching the Big Bad Wolf. It was lucky you were here when he showed up."

"I wish we could stay here," sighed Jasmine. "I don't want to go back to our world."

Trixi frowned. "Why not?"

Jasmine explained about the school play. "I don't want to be in it any more," she said. "Not after messing up my dance."

"Ooh, can you show me your dance?" asked Trixi. "I'd love to see it."

"I suppose so," Jasmine said in a gloomy voice. "If I can remember it." She moved into a space and Ellie began to hum the dance tune.

Jasmine stretched up on tiptoe, then
twirled gracefully from side to side.
A group of unicorns came to watch,
nodding their heads with approval. Other
magical creatures gathered round, too.

When the dance was over, everyone
clapped enthusiastically.

"Wow!" Trixi exclaimed, clapping her tiny hands. "That looked perfect to me."

"Yes, but I'm wearing a magic tutu," Jasmine said. "If I could take it home with me and wear it on stage I'd be able to dance brilliantly, but I can't. I'm going to get it all wrong again and ruin the show!"

Grandmother Aura stepped out of the crowd. "But, Jasmine! I forgot to tell you – there's no magic in your costume! I was just about to start sewing it in when the wolf came."

Jasmine gazed at her in astonishment. "So you mean...?"

"That dance was all your own work," Grandmother Aura said.

Jasmine beamed at her. "That's great! It means I *do* know the dance after all!"

"So are you ready to go home now?" asked Trixi.

"Definitely," replied Jasmine. "I can hardly wait to get back to our rehearsal. I'm going to perform my dance without any mistakes this time!"

"Good for you," Summer said, smiling.

"We knew you could do it, Jasmine," said Ellie.

The three girls joined hands. "There's only one more fairytale baddie to find now," said Summer as they waited for Trixi to perform her magic.

Trixi tapped her ring and a shower of multicoloured sparkles came fizzing out. "Goodbye, girls," she said.

"Goodbye, Trixi. See you again soon," Summer said, as the sparkles closed in tight around the girls.

"Here we go!" cried Ellie as they felt themselves being lifted off their feet.

A moment later the sparkles faded to nothing and they were back in the dressing room at school once more. Their costumes had vanished – Ellie and Summer were dressed in their normal clothes, and Jasmine was wearing her Cinderella costume again.

"That was quite an adventure!" said Jasmine.

"But we did it," Ellie said happily.

"I can't wait to go back to the Secret Kingdom," Summer said. "I hope Trixi calls us again soon."

"Me too!" cried Ellie and Jasmine together.

"But first we've got a rehearsal to finish," said Jasmine. "Let's go and show everyone my dance!" Smiling, the three friends joined hands and skipped off together towards the school hall.

In the next Secret Kingdom adventure, Ellie, Summer and Jasmine visit

Jewel Cavern

Read on for a sneak peek...

A Secret Message

"Gather round everyone!" Mrs Benson called. "In this glass case you'll see a very precious gold and emerald tiara. Come and look!"

Summer, Ellie and Jasmine joined their classmates around the big museum display case. "Oh, wow." Jasmine said, looking at the glittering tiara inside. "I love school trips – this is so much better than being in maths!"

Ellie nodded. "It's really beautiful." She turned to a clean page on her notebook and started to sketch the tiara.

Summer leaned closer. "It *is* lovely," she agreed in a whisper. "But not as pretty as *our* tiaras!"

The three girls grinned at each other. They had an amazing secret. They were the special helpers of an enchanted land called the Secret Kingdom. The kingdom was an incredible place full of magical creatures, but it had a terrible problem. The leader of the land, kindly King Merry, had a horrible sister who was trying to take over and make everyone as miserable as she was. Luckily, King Merry had invented a magic box that had found the only people that could help – Summer, Jasmine and Ellie!

Ever since they'd found the Magic Box at their school fete, they'd been going to the kingdom whenever horrid Queen Malice caused trouble. When they were needed, a riddle would appear in the mirror of the Magic Box, and Trixibelle, their pixie friend, would appear to whisk them away to the amazing crescent-moon shaped island.

As soon as they got there, beautiful tiaras appeared on their heads to show everyone that they were Very Important Friends of King Merry.

Mrs Benson clapped her hands. "Right, it's time to go into the next room now. This way, everyone!" She swept off, leading the class into a room where a huge dinosaur skeleton towered up to the ceiling.

"Shall we check the Magic Box?" Jasmine whispered.

Summer and Ellie nodded and they hung back as the class went through to the dinosaur room. They never knew when they might get a message from their friends, so they took it in turns taking the Magic Box with them wherever they went. Ellie had brought it on the school trip in her backpack.

Queen Malice's latest nasty plan had been to release six baddies from Summer's fairytale book into the land. The queen hoped they would cause so much chaos that everyone would beg her to take over as ruler instead of King Merry. So far, the girls had captured five of the baddies she had released – a witch, a wizard, an ogre, a giant and a big bad wolf, but there was still one left on the loose...

Read

Jewel Cavern

to find out what
happens next!

Secret Kingdom

Have you read all the books in Series 3?

Wildflower Wood
ROSIE BANKS

Swan Palace
ROSIE BANKS

Snow Bear Sanctuary
ROSIE BANKS

Phoenix Festival
ROSIE BANKS

Fancy Dress Party
ROSIE BANKS

Jewel Tavern
ROSIE BANKS

Enjoy six sparkling adventures!

Secret Kingdom

Be in on the secret. Collect them all!

Series 1

When Jasmine, Summer and Ellie discover the magical land of the Secret Kingdom, a whole world of adventure awaits!

Series 2

Wicked Queen Malice has cast a spell to
turn King Merry into a toad! Can the girls
find six magic ingredients to save him?

Look out for the next sparkling series!

In Series 4,
meet the magical Animal Keepers of the
Secret Kingdom, who spread fun, friendship,
kindness and bravery throughout the land!

When wicked Queen Malice casts an evil spell
to reverse the Keepers' powers, it's up to Ellie,
Summer and Jasmine to find each animal's
magical charm and reunite them with their
Keeper – before their special values disappear
from the kingdom forever!

Available
February 2014

The Animal Keepers of the Secret Kingdom
live in a magical shield in King Merry's Enchanted
Palace, and are brought to life every hundred
years to spread fun, friendship, kindness and
bravery throughout the land.

Design your own Keepers shield in the space above.
Choose any animals you like – real or magical!

Competition!

Evil Queen Malice has been up to no good again and hidden six of her naughty Storm Sprites in the pages of each Secret Kingdom book in series three!

Did you spot the Storm Sprite while you were reading this book?

Ellie, Summer and Jasmine need your help!

Can you find the pages where the cheeky Sprites are hiding in each of the six books in series three?

When you have found all six Storm Sprites, go online and tell us what pages they are hiding on and enter the competition at

www.secretkingdombooks.com

We will put all of the correct entries into a draw and select one winner to receive a special Secret Kingdom goodie bag featuring lots of sparkly gifts, including a glittery t-shirt!